What Will the Weather Be?

Diane Cox

D1369861

Rigby

What will the weather be? I can use these signs and a weather map to help me plan each day.

cloudy

sunny

snowy

windy

stormy

Spring

I live in Springfield. My friend and I want to play shadow tag today. Will the sun shine?

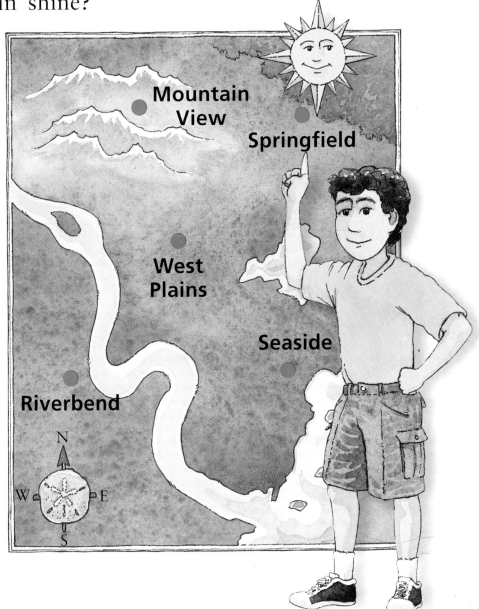

The  on the map means it will be sunny. We can play shadow tag.

Summer

We are going camping at Riverbend. We want to look at the stars. Will the sky be clear tonight?

The  means it will be cloudy.
We won't be able to see the stars.
Could we roast marshmallows instead?

Fall

I am visiting my cousin in Seaside today. We want to fly my kite. Will the wind blow today?

The  means it will be windy.
We can fly my kite.

Winter

We are going to Mountain View. I want to build a snowman. Will there be snow?

The  means it will snow.
I can build a snowman.

Spring

We want to go to the theme park at West Plains. Would today be a good day to go?

The  means it will be stormy.
We won't go today.

Summer

We want to have a picnic at the beach today. I can use a weather map to help plan my day.

Weather maps are helpful.

But sometimes the weather can change fast!

Index

 cloudy   2, 5–6

 snowy   2, 9–10

 stormy   2, 11–12

 sunny   2, 3–4

 windy   2, 7–8